Percussion Players

Simple activities for using percussion in the classroom

Compiled and written by
Jane Sebba

Illustrated by
Alison Dexter

With additional activities by
Uchenna Ngwe

A&C Black • London

Audio track list

Musical games

Sort it out! | 1. C major scale

High, low, middle
2. High, low, middle performance
3. CCF (slowly)
4. High, low, middle

Which notes are these?
5. Which notes are these? performance
6. Which notes are these? performance with gap

What are you wearing?
7. What are you wearing? performance

I went to market...
8. I went to market performance

Ostinato accompaniments

London's burning
9. London's burning performance
10. Tuned ostinato
11. Untuned ostinato
12. Backing track

Frère Jacques
13. Frère Jacques performance
14. Tuned ostinato
15. Untuned ostinato
16. Backing track

Row, row, row your boat
17. Row, row, row your boat performance
18. Tuned ostinato
19. Untuned ostinato
20. Backing track

A sailor went to sea
21. A sailor went to sea performance
22. Tuned ostinato and chords
23. Backing track

Swing low, sweet chariot
24. Swing low performance
25. Tuned ostinato
26. Untuned ostinato
27. Backing track

Mango walk
28. Mango walk performance
29. Tuned and untuned ostinato
30. Backing track

Sarasponda
31. Sarasponda performance
32. Untuned and tuned ostinato
33. Backing track

Chord accompaniments

What shall we play?
34. What shall we play? performance
35. Backing track

John Brown's brother
36. John Brown's brother performance
37. Backing track

My bonnie
38. My bonnie performance
39. Backing track

Simple gifts
40. Simple gifts performance
41. Backing track

Daisy bell
42. Daisy bell performance
43. Backing track

Pokarekare ana
44. Pokarekare ana performance
45. Pokarekare ana copy track
46. Backing track

Greensleeves
47. Greensleeves performance
48. Backing track

Sambalele
49. Sambalele performance
50. Untuned ostinato
51. Tuned ostinato
52. Backing track

Tunes to play

Suo-gân
53. Suo-gân performance
54. Backing track

Land of the silver birch
55. Land of the silver birch performance
56. Tuned ostinato
57. Untuned ostinato
58. Backing track

Oh, when the saints
59. When the saints performance
60. Backing track

All the pretty horses
61. All the pretty horses performance
62. Backing track

Migldi magldi
63. Migldi magldi performance
64. Backing track

Composing

A musical sandwich
65. A musical sandwich performance

Secrets of the animal kingdom
66. Secrets of the animal kingdom

Contents

Using the pack

Music Express EXTRA: *Percussion Players* uses accessible percussion to develop musicianship, pitch, rhythm and composition in the classroom. Performing as a group using voice and percussion is not only great fun but an integral part of musical development.

This easy-to-follow resource uses well-known songs in fresh, engaging activities and breathes new life into traditional classroom instruments. Developed with classroom teaching in mind, the material throughout *Percussion Players* can be taught by an experienced or a less musically-confident teacher.

HOW THE PACK IS ORGANISED AND WHAT YOU NEED

Percussion Players is a multimedia resource comprising three components – a book, an audio CD (containing performance and backing tracks) and a CD ROM (containing activities for use with an interactive whiteboard or computer, and photocopiable printouts). The pack can be used in a number of ways: as a dip-in resource, as a source of group warm-ups or to enhance an existing scheme of work. However you use it, *Percussion Players* will inspire you and your class to get out those instruments and start having fun with percussion!

BOOK

The book has six sections: Musical games, Ostinato accompaniments, Chord accompaniments, Tunes to play, Composing and Example Printouts. A full list of printouts can be downloaded from the CD ROM. At the back of the book are notated melody lines and chords. As an additional teaching aid you may handwrite song lyrics to display on an OHP or whiteboard.

Most of the activities have a 'What you will need' box and a 'Teaching tip' (see opposite). These boxes contain information of all the materials and resources necessary to perform the activity successfully.

CD/CD-ROMs

The two CD/CD ROMs are both enhanced CDs. Use them in a conventional CD player in order to play the audio tracks. Use them on a computer/whiteboard set-up to show the children the whiteboard displays or to make printouts.

 CD track numbers used for the activity. See audio track list page 2.

Interactive whiteboard activity number. Printouts for performance actvities can be downloaded from the CD ROM.

What you will need

- Any tuned percussion instrument with these notes:

  D G A B D'

- A variety of beaters.

Teaching tip
Create a hand signal which means that the whole class must be still and silent. It could be raising your hnnds in the air or putting them on your head!

Classroom music making

The task of organising a large group or several smaller groups in a percussion activity can be daunting for a teacher. There are however ways that classroom music making with percussion can be enjoyable and productive for all. Without having to read a note of music, your class can benefit from a tuneful and educational musical experience that both you and they will enjoy. Here are some pointers to make music lessons run as smoothly as possible:

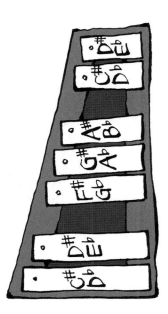

1. Successful music-making is often a product of good teamwork. Just as football players must be aware of the other members of the team, so must musicians be aware of and listen to others in order to play together as a team.

   Tell your class that in order to be good musicians it is important that they listen to others. Listening is a skill in its own right and some children will find it difficult at first. Also, point out that playing a musical piece is not a race to finish first.

2. When you give a child a percussion instrument, (s)he will want to play with it - and the effect is often noisy! It is very difficult to give clear instructions for a musical performance to the class when several children are playing percussion instruments at once. It is therefore advisable to establish some ground rules for when to be silent. Make a rule that instruments and beaters should be placed on the floor or table when not in use.

3. Silence is an important componant of music. Encourage the performers to be still like statues at the beginning and at the end of their pieces. Listeners should always be quiet while others perform - and performers should give their audience something worth being quiet for!

4. When combining voice and tuned percussion it is important to all begin singing on the correct note. To demonstrate the starting note with the class either familiarise yourself with the recording or play the first note on a tuned instrument.

   The alto xylophone is closest in range to children's voices, so if you have one, use it for giving starting notes. If you find it difficult to reproduce notes vocally, delegate the job to someone in your class for whom it is easy.

5. For each item that includes a song or chant, a steady pulse should be established. You can take the pulse from the relevant track on the recording. Take a moment to establish the speed of the song or chant in your head, then count aloud to bring everyone in together (it may help to use clapping to demonstrate the beat to the class). Tell the children beforehand what you are going to count and when they should start singing, this will help the class to perform at the same speed.

Instruments

Tuned percussion instruments

The tuned percussion instruments referred to in this book are the most commonly used ones – xylophones, glockenspiels, metallophones and chime bars, although others such as steel pans, vibraphones and tubular bells may be used if available.

Tuned instruments are so called because when struck, usually with a beater, they make a definite note or pitch (e g, **C D E**).

Tuned instruments provide a perfect visual aid for teaching children about pitch in music as their note bars are arranged so neatly and satisfactorily. With the name of the notes marked on each bar and the size and position of each note clearly visible, even children who find abstract concepts hard to grasp will understand the principles of high and low.

Each bar is clearly labelled with the note that it plays (for the note **C**, strike the bar labelled **C**). You will notice that each bar varies in length – longer bars have a lower pitch and shorter bars have a higher pitch.

On a tuned instrument you can literally play a tune. Try the beginning of *Frère Jacques*:

C D E C C D E C

Beaters

There are different types of beaters – wooden, plastic, rubber or soft felt. The sound produced on a tuned percussion instrument varies according to the beater used.

Family members

Glockenspiels, xylophones, metallophones and chime bar sets are available in different sizes. The smallest are called soprano instruments and produce the highest notes. The next lowest in pitch are called the alto, followed by the tenor. The lowest (and largest) instrument is called the bass. The alto instruments are closest in range to children's voices and should be used if available.

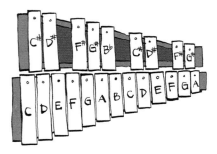

Range

The musical note names **A B C D E F G** are the first seven notes of the alphabet. There is no H note but instead the sequence of letters repeats. Therefore you may see two bars labelled **C** but the bars are different lengths. This is because it is a higher or lower version of the same note (remember, if the bar is shorter it will be higher).

Throughout the book you will see letters with dashes next to them (**C'**). A dash above the note means that it is the higher version, no dash at all (**C**) means that it is mid-range, and a dash below the note (**C,**) means that it is a lower version of the note. To make this clearer:

C,	C	C'
Low	**Middle**	**High**

Recognising percussion instruments

The name xylophone comes from the Greek meaning wood sound. Xylophones have wooden bars that rest on a deep wooden resonator box. In German, the word *glocken* means bells and *spiel* means play. Glockenspiels have narrow, metal bars which sound bell-like when played. Metallophones also have metal bars as their name suggests, however they are thicker than those on a glockenspiel. A chime bar is a single bar mounted on its own resonating box.

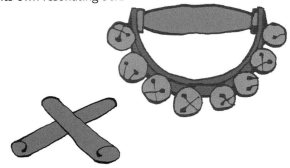

Untuned percussion

Tambourines, bells, woodblocks, cymbals and many types of drums are all common examples of untuned percussion in the classroom. They are known as untuned because the sound that they make when played has no definite pitch or note (you cannot play **C D E** for *Frère Jacques* on a tambourine, as you can on a xylophone).

Musical games

<table>
<tr></tr>
</table>

What you will need

- Any tuned percussion instrument.
- A collection of objects which may make a sound, eg a bunch of keys, a comb.
- A variety of beaters preferably made from different materials - wooden, plastic, rubber.

Teaching tip

More ideas for making sounds:

Strike a note bar with a key;

Use pens or pencils as beaters;

Fill a bag with lentils and tap on the note bars.

WHAT YOU NEED TO KNOW ABOUT THE STARTER ACTIVITY
Ways to play

This is a game for exploring sound quality (known as *timbre* or *tone* in music) using all the notes of a tuned percussion instrument and various other objects. It allows the children to discover the resonating properties of the instrument.

Children should explore and discover the different sound qualities of various tuned percussion instruments.

1. Position the collection of tuned instruments and objects so that the entire class can see them.

2. Explore the different sounds made when the note bars are struck with different objects. Discuss the difference in sounds.

3. Each child looks for original ways to play. Encourage the children to experiment and to be inventive, taking care not to damage the instruments.

Here are some ideas for making sounds:

bounce a ping pong ball on the note bars;

blow over the note bars;

pull a comb across the edge of a note bar;

tap or drag fingernails or knuckles across the note bars;

strike a note bar with a beater, then stop the sound immediately by touching the note bar with a finger;

stike a note bar with a beater and touch it with a key while it is still vibrating.

★ Extend the activity

Add other instruments and position them along with the objects and a player behind a screen. The children who are listening guess the instrument as well as describing how they think the sound is being made.

Sort it out!

WHAT YOU NEED TO KNOW ABOUT SORT IT OUT!

The aim of this musical game is to order eight jumbled notes from lowest to highest in step starting on **C** and finishing on **C'**. The notes in the activity are **C D E F G A B C'**. In music this is known as the C major scale (see Teaching tip). Notice how the note bars become shorter as the note sounds higher.

Play sort it out!

1. Listen to track 1 and/or play the notes **C D E F G A B C'** (in that order) to the class on a xylophone or glockenspiel. Invite the class to join in with you by singing the note names in order as you play. Play and sing the eight notes together until the whole class is confident.

2. Choose eight volunteers to stand in a line with their backs to the class. Mix up the order of the chime bars and give one to each child.

3. Ask each volunteer to play their note in turn beginning with the person on the left (of the class).

4. Listen to track 1 and/or play **C D E F G A B C'** (the C major scale) on the xylophone again to remind your class. Allow the children to take turns to reorder the jumbled chime bars into the correct order to make a C major scale. The volunteers should repeat their notes as many times as is necessary to help their classmates find the correct order of the C major scale.

★ Extend the activity

Once the class can confidently recognise and play the C major scale ascending (going upwards in step between **C** and **C'**) repeat the *Sort it out!* game but this time ordering the notes from high (**C'**) to low (**C**) in step to create a descending C major scale (see Teaching tip).

★ Get interactive

Two variations of the *Sort it out!* game can be played on the interactive whiteboard and on classroom computers, *Sort it out!* and *Sort it out! (find the notes)*. Play the CD ROM and choose musical game number 1 or 2. Follow the instructions in the Help box. The children must first arrange the illustrations into the correct order from low to high to form the C major scale and then recognise the notes of the C major scale when they are hidden from view.

What you will need

- A xylophone, glockenspiel or metallophone.
- These chime bar notes;

C D E F G A B C'

- Eight beaters.
- Eight players.
- CD ROM activities - *Sort it out!* and *Sort it out! (find the notes)*.

Teaching tip

Eight notes which move from low to high is an ASCENDING SCALE. In *Sort it out!* the children learn the ascending scale of C major:

C D E F G A B C'

Therefore eight notes which move from high to low is a DESCENDING SCALE. A descending C major scale would be played;

C' B A G F E D C

Simon Says

What you will need

- A tuned percussion instrument with these notes:

  D D'

- If you wish to play the extended version of *Simon Says*, you will need an assortment of different notes.

WHAT YOU NEED TO KNOW ABOUT SIMON SAYS

In this musical version of the popular game *Simon says*, the children respond to notes of different pitches: **D** and **D'**. The lower note (**D**) indicates that the children should follow the instruction, and the higher note (**D'**) indicates that they must remain still.

Play Simon Says

1. Tell the class that you are going to be Simon. Remind the class of the rules to the game *Simon Says* - that 'Simon' gives instructions and the class must follow but only if you say 'Simon says....' before the instruction, like so:

Say 'Simon says stand up' - everyone should stand up.

Say 'Simon says put your hands on you head' - everyone should put their hands on their heads.

Say 'Sit down' - anyone who sits down is out of the game, because you did not say 'Simon says' before the instruction.

2. Continue the game with different instructions. Remember to say 'Simon says' only sometimes before the instructions.

Play Simon Says using percussion

1. Position an instrument (eg xylophone, glockenspiel) so that it is hidden from view. First demonstrate the note which tells the children to perform what Simon says (low **D**) and then demonstrate the note which tells them to ignore Simon's instruction (high **D'**). Play as many times as necessary until the class is confident.

2. Play **D** followed by an instruction. Everyone should perform the action (because it was the lower of the two notes). Repeat this as many times as you like, giving a new instruction every time.

3. Play **D'** and then give another instruction. The children should remain still (because it was the higher of the two notes). Anyone who doesn't is out of the game.

★ Extend the activity

Play the game with a different pair of notes with smaller or larger intervals, eg, **C** and **E**.

Choose two children to play the part of Simon. One plays the notes and the other performs an action for the children to copy.

Teaching tip

An interval is the space between two notes. The space between C and A is a large interval (6th) however the space between notes C and D is a small interval (2nd).

High, low, middle

WHAT YOU NEED TO KNOW ABOUT HIGH, LOW, MIDDLE

High, low, middle is sung to the well-known tune *Hot cross buns*. The first three notes of *Hot cross buns* are **C' C F** (High, low middle) which are used in the game. A child chooses a new sequence for the three notes, eg **F C C'** (middle, low, high) which is then used to create a new last line for the song. An interactive version of this game is on the CD ROM, activity 3.

1. Teach *High, low, middle* using track 2.

(**First version**)

High, low, middle.

High, low, middle.

Change the order of the notes from

High, low, middle.

(**Second version**)

High, low, middle.

High, low, middle.

Change the order of the notes to

Middle, low, high.

2. Teach the tuned percussion part (**C' F C** and **F C C'**). Use track 3 to help. Children should play along with the last line of each verse.

3. Listen to track 4. Discuss what is different in this version. Choose a child to change the last line of the song using the words high, low or middle to describe the relative pitches. You can repeat the same word (note) twice if you want to, eg, *high, high, low*. Keep choosing different end sequences and sing them together as a class.

 2-4 WB

• A tuned percussion instrument with these notes:

C F C'

• CD ROM activity - *High, low middle.*

Teaching tip
Encourage the whole class or small groups to show the relative pitches (high, low and middle) using their hands (see illustration below).

High,   low,   middle.

high

low

middle

High, low, middle

Teaching tip
As you extend the activity further it is important to keep reminding the children of the three notes for high, low, middle, C' F C. You can do this using a tuned percussion instrument or by listening to track 3. Remember that you can use the same note twice eg, high, high, low or low, middle, low.

4. Now ask a volunteer to make up a new ending to the song by playing the last three notes in a new order on a tuned percussion instrument. Encourage them to identify the pitches using the words high, low, middle.

Questions you might ask

What are the words **high**, **low** and **middle** describing?
(answer: the pitch of the notes - how high or low it is).

What do the class think the song is asking them to do in this game?
(answer: to change the order of the pitches of the notes in the last line of the song and sing or play them).

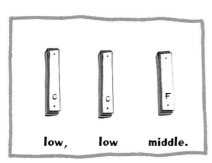

low, low middle.

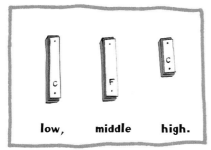

low, middle high.

★ Extend the activity

Divide the class into two groups. One half of the class sing, while the others join in using tuned instruments for the last lines of the verses. Remember that **C'** should be played for the word 'high', **F** for 'middle' and **C** for 'low'. The singers can do the actions (see illustrations) while singing.

★ A variation of the game is to divide the class into three. One group could be 'high' and sing **C'**, the second could be 'middle' and sing **F'** and the third group 'low' and sing **C**. Assign one child as conductor. When the last line of the song arrives the conductor points to the groups in the order that they must sing eg, middle, high, low. They must be quick off the mark and sing the correct note! Some children in each group might have tuned percussion and play their note rather than sing it.

★ One child plays a sequence of the three notes while the others in the group cover their eyes. They must identify the correct sequence of notes by listening only (eg, middle, middle, high).

low

middle

Which notes are these?

WHAT YOU NEED TO KNOW ABOUT WHICH NOTES ARE THESE?

This song is sung to the tune *Who built the ark?* A child makes up a four note melody to take the place of the second line using the F pentatonic scale (**F G A C' D'** - see Teaching tip). The other children identify those four notes using tuned percussion and by listening carefully.

1. Teach the class *Which notes are these?* using track 5 until the class is familiar with the tune and lyrics.

2. Ask the children to clap the four beats in the second line of the song. Use an untuned percussion instrument such as a drum or tambourine to outline the four strong beats in line two. Use track 6 to demonstrate.

   Which notes are these?

   X   X   X   X

   Which notes are these?

   Can you tell me what they are?

3. Listen to track 5 again. Tell the class that the melody played in the second line is made up of two notes, **F** and **A**. Once the class is familiar with the notes, give out chime bars, xylophones or glockenspiels and play along with the song (see below).

   Which notes are these?

   A   F   A   F

   Which notes are these?

   Can you tell me what they are?

Teaching tip
A pentatonic scale is made up of five different notes. The F pentatonic scale which is used in this musical game includes the notes:

F G A C' D'

4. Choose a child to be the player. Place the instrument where the other children can't see it. The player chooses four notes from **F G A C' D'** (the F pentatonic scale) and plays them in place of the four hand claps. This is the second line of the song. The rest of the class sing the other three lines. The player can repeat the same note twice in his/her sequence.

   Which notes are these?

   ? ? ? ?

   Which notes are these?

   Can you tell me what they are?

Which notes are these?

5. After listening to the new notes played by the player in the second line the children must try to guess what the notes are. Remember they can only be from the F pentatonic scale - **F G A C' D'**. An example might be:

Which notes are these?

F   A   F   D'

Which notes are these?
Can you tell me what they are?

The player must repeat the four notes as many times as necessary to help the rest of the class identify the notes. Allow the children to use tuned instruments to help.

★ Extend the activity

Allow the children to play any notes from the F pentatonic scale, making sure that they still fit into the gap. Remember that the F pentatonic scale is made up of five notes, **F G A C' D'**.

Give some children untuned percussion instruments so that they can join in and beat the pulse and sing the entire song with the rest of the class. They may wish to particularly emphaise the four beats of the second line.

★ Get interactive

Which notes are these? is activity 4 on the CD Rom. This interactive activity tests the children's listening and identifying skils. Four random notes play in the second line and the children use the xylophone on screen to identify which notes they are.

A xylophone showing the notes of the **F pentatonic scale F G A C' D'**.

These are the notes the children choose from to create line two of *Which notes are these?*

What are you wearing?

WHAT YOU NEED TO KNOW ABOUT WHAT ARE YOU WEARING?

The children think of items of clothing and use the word rhythms (see Teaching tip) to make tunes that are ascending (moving up by step) or descending (moving down by step), ending on a high **C'** or a low **C**.

1. Teach the chant *What are you wearing?* using track 7.

    The clothes in grey (below) are on the track but are those that the children will change to create their own lines once they are confident with the game.

    What are you wearing?

    Dungarees or skirt,

    Stripes or spots

    or a plain white shirt?

    What are you wearing?

    Black shoes

    What are you wearing?

    Black shoes

    What are you wearing? Dungarees or skirt,

    Stripes or spots or a plain white shirt?

    What are you wearing?

    Two stripy gloves.

    What are you wearing?

    Two stripy gloves.

What you will need

 7)))

- A tuned percussion instrument with these notes:

    C D E F G A B C'

Teaching tip

A word rhythm is the rhythm that the word has when spoken. In this musical game each syllable of the word should be played as a note ascending or descending between low C and high C.

Two	stri-py		gloves
x	x	x	x

For those practitioners with knowledge of musical notation the word rhythms for this chant are:

♩ ♫ ♩ 𝄽

Two   stri-py   gloves.

♩ 𝄽 ♩ 𝄽

Black   shoes

What are you wearing?

Other word rhythms

There are many items of clothing that the children can put into the chant - the more creative the better! Here are a few ideas to start them off:

Pink   Py-   jam- as

Pur- ple   boots

Or-   ange   jeans

Green and yell-ow socks

2. Sing the song *What are you wearing?* as a class. Clap along a steady beat in time with the song. When the class is confident invite individuals to beat with untuned percussion instruments such as wood blocks, tambourines or bells.

3. Discuss new replies to the question 'What are you wearing?' and perform them as a class. Ideas might be 'a yellow T-shirt' or 'a pair of brown shoes' (see 'other word rhythms' box).

4. The children can now play the word rhythms of the clothes on a tuned percussion instrument as an answer to the question 'what are you wearing?'. They can choose any notes between **C** and **C'** ascending or descending. An example might be:

What are you wearing?

E   F   G   B

Two   str- ipy   gloves.

5. Now teach the children how to play the question 'What are you wearing?'

C'   F   D'   C'   F

What   **are** **you**   **wear-** **ing?**

★ Extend the activity

It is now possible for some of the children to play the question (What are you wearing?'), some to play the answer (eg. 'two stri-py gloves) and others to play the beat on untuned percussion and sing along.

More confident children can perform their own answers individually using tuned percussion or their voice.

t to market

NEED TO KNOW ABOUT I WENT TO MARKET

l version of the game I went to market and I bought..., the children... of words beginning with the note names **A**, **B**, **C D E F G** and **A**. After each item they use the notes to play the word rhythm (see explanation of word rhythms on pg 14). Remember that all words in grey (below) are those which can be changed by the children once they are confident with the rules of the game.

I. Listen to track 8 and become familiar with the format of this game. It is extremely important that you are absolutely certain of the rules of 'I went to market and I bought...' before you introduce the game to the class. Listen to track 8 as many times as necessary.

> **I went to market and I bought**
>> an armadillo
>>
>> A, A, A, A,
>>
>> (ar-ma-dil-lo)

> **I went to market and I bought**
>> an armadillo
>>
>> A, A, A, ,A
>>
>> **and** a biscuit
>>
>> B, B,
>>
>> (bi-scuit)

2. Teach the game to the children. With each verse a different item is added to the shopping list which begins with the next note letter in the sequence from **A**, to **G**.

> **I went to market and I bought**
>> an armadillo
>>
>> A, A, A, A,
>>
>> **and** a biscuit
>>
>> B, B,
>>
>> **and** a catapult
>>
>> C C C
>>
>> (cat-a-pult)
>>
>> **and** a dog
>>
>> D
>>
>> (dog)

I went to market

and an egg

E

(egg)

and a feather

F F

(feather)

and a goldfish

G G

(goldfish)

and an apple pie

A A A

(apple pie)

3. Once items beginning with **A**, to **G** have been sung, items are given back in reverse order and others are kept.

   I don't like apple pie

   A A A

   so I gave that back, but I kept the

   goldfish

   G G

   and the feather

   F F

   and the egg

   E

4. The whole class sit in a circle. Place the tuned percussion instrument (eg, xylophone, glockenspiel or metallophone) in the middle so that it can be seen by everybody. Ask a volunteer to begin the game by saying 'I went to market and I bought...' choosing a word beginning with the letter A for the list. They then play the rhythm of the word on the note **A**,.This is the lower A note (two notes below **C**)

5. As more children perform, continue adding and playing new words beginning with the remaining letters **B C D E F G** and **A**.

6. The next child says 'I don't like...' and says and plays the rhythm of the word thought of by the previous child. The rest of the words are then said and performed in reverse order by the next children (the notes going down instead of up).

7. The children copy the format of the game on the CD but add their own items, which means new word rhythms.

Ostinato accompaniments

Playing ostinato accompaniments to songs is an effective and simple way to create an interesting classroom performance using any percussion instrument you can find.

What is an ostinato?

An *ostinato* (plural – *ostinati*) is a repeated musical pattern. This is simply a pattern of notes repeated over and over again to accompany a song, eg,

G D G   G D G

In order for an ostinato to fit successfully with a song, the performer must play the pattern strictly in time to the beat. Some ostinato patterns used in this book copy short lines or phrases taken from the songs, making them very easy to learn. Action patterns are used to great effect to teach ostinati. The children become confident with the actions before they replace them with tuned percussion instruments and use beaters to make the sound (see Teaching Tip).

Working with ostinati

In this book two types of ostinato patterns are used – tuned (using tuned percussion instruments, eg, xylophones) and untuned (using untuned percussion instruments, eg, tambourines).

To perform a song with an ostinato the class must be aware of two musical ideas at once: the song and the ostinato. It is extremely important that everyone learns the song thoroughly before adding the ostinato.

For most of the songs, there are suggestions for additional ostinato patterns to play on untuned instruments. Each of these follows a short rhythm taken from the song.

Untuned ostinato

- Practise the untuned ostinato on its own.

- Practise performing the untuned ostinato with the song.

- Ensure that the children can confidently perform the song with the untuned ostinato accompaniment.

Tuned ostinato

- Play the tuned ostinato once as an introduction and continue playing while the song is performed over it – try again with untuned ostinato. Which one sounds best?

- Begin both the tuned ostinato and the song together.

- Perform the untuned ostinato part, the tuned ostinato part and the song simultaneously.

  Can anybody think of any other ways to perform the songs?

As there may be up to three parts being performed at once, be sure that you are very familiar with all of them. You may like to appoint a leader for each group. Remind the children that when they are performing, they are all pieces in a musical jigsaw that must fit together neatly. The audio CD has all parts as well as performance and backing tracks. It is a great idea to keep referring back to the CD in order to learn every part. Make sure that the children can see a printout of their part until it is learnt.

Get interactive

Every song in *Percussion Players* with ostinato accompaniments has an interactive performance activity on the CD ROM. This enables the class to watch the lyrics of the song and the tuned ostinato as the song plays. Each activity has a printout of the tuned and untuned percussion parts. There are example printouts in the book also. At the bottom of each printout is a simplified version of the ostinato pattern.

You can print the ostinato parts and give them to the class, so that they can play along with the interactive activity.

The interactive performance activities on the CD ROM only include one verse of the song so that the children can practise the tuned percussion pattern. Use the printouts and the audio CD for a full performance with the entire class.

Teaching tip

In *Percussion Players* the ostinato patterns (particularly the tuned ostinato) are taught using action patterns. These are a series of actions, such as clapping, bending and knee tapping, which teach the rhythm of the ostinato until the children are confident enough to add the tuned percussion instrument.

London's burning

What you will need

 9 -12)))

- tuned percussion instruments (eg, xylophones) with these notes:

  D G

- some untuned percussion instruments. eg tambourines, woodblocks, maracas.
- CD ROM activity and printout - *London's burning*.

The class sing *London's burning* and accompany the song with two ostinato patterns, one for tuned percussion and one for untuned percussion. The tuned ostinato pattern is learned using an action pattern which reflects the high and low notes.

1. Teach the song *London's burning* using track 9.

   London's burning, London's burning,

   fetch the engines, fetch the engines.

   Fire, fire! Fire, fire!

   Pour on water, pour on water.

2. Teach the action pattern (below) and repeat until secure. Each action should be performed with each syllable. The bent action represents the lower note on the tuned percussion, and the standing action represents the higher note.

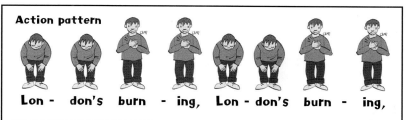

Divide the children into two groups; one group sings the song while the other performs the action pattern. When confident, swap parts and perform again.

3. Learn the tuned ostinato part using track 10 and the CD ROM activity.

Tuned ostinato pattern

D	D	G	G	D	D	G	G
Lon -	don's	burn	- ing,	Lon -	don's	burn	- ing,

A small group can play the tuned ostinato while the rest of the class sing. Divide the class into three groups; one to sing, one to perform the action pattern and one to play the tuned ostinato. When secure, swap until all children have performed each part.

4. Learn the untuned ostinato part using track 11.

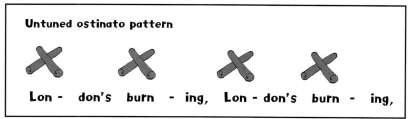

5. Divide the children into three groups: one to sing, one to play the tuned ostinato and one to play the untuned ostinato. Perform to the backing track (track 12). Use the printouts on the CD ROM to learn parts.

Teaching tip

It may help the children performing the action pattern part to repeat the words 'London's burning' over and over while the others sing and play percussion.

Frère Jacques

After singing *Frère Jacques*, the children learn tuned percussion and untuned percussion ostinato patterns to accompany the song. The tuned ostinato is taught using a simple action pattern.

1. Learn the song *Frère Jacques* using track 13.

> **Frère Jacques, Frère Jacques,**
>
> **dormez vous? dormez vous?**
>
> **Sonnez les matines, sonnez les matines,**
>
> **Din, dan don. Din, dan, don.**

2. Teach the children the action pattern (below) and repeat using track 13 until secure.

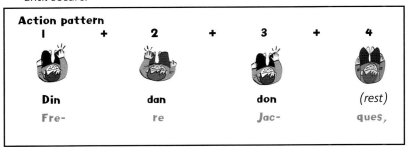

Divide the class into two groups; one sings the song while the other repeats the action pattern throughout. Swap groups and repeat until everyone has performed both parts.

3. Learn the tuned percussion ostinato part (below) using track 14 and the CD ROM.

Tuned ostinato pattern							
1	**+**	**2**	**+**	**3**	**+**	**4**	
F		C		F		(rest)	
Din		**dan**		**don**		(rest)	
Frè-		re		Jac-		ques,	

A small group can play the tuned ostinato while the rest of the class sing.

Divide the class into three groups; one to sing, one to perform the action pattern and one to play the tuned ostinato. When secure, swap until all children have performed each part.

4. Invite a small group to play the word-rhythm that fits with the line *Sonnez les matines* (below). Encourage the rest of the class to clap the beat softly to help them.

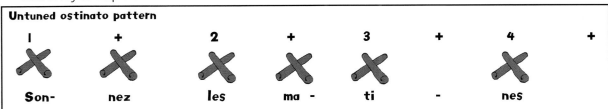

5. Divide the children into three groups: one to sing, one to play the tuned percussion ostinato and one to play the untuned percussion ostinato. Perform with the backing track (track 16).

What you will need

 13-16)))

- tuned percussion instruments (eg, xylophones) with these notes:

  C F

- some untuned percussion instruments. eg tambourines, woodblocks, maracas.

- CD ROM activity and printout - *Frère Jacques*.

Teacher's Tip

Notice which hands play each note in the tuned ostinato (the right hand plays F and the left hand plays C,). All practice playing along with the recording on imaginary beaters.

Row, row, row your boat

What you will need

 17-20))) WB

- tuned percussion instruments (eg, xylophones) with these notes:

  C E G C'

- some untuned percussion instruments. eg tambourines, woodblocks, maracas.
- CD ROM activity and printout - *Row your boat.*

Teacher's Tip

Choose a leader to help the tuned ostinato group by performing the action pattern in front of them as a memory aid once they have moved onto using the instruments.

The children sing and play a tuned ostinato which fits the phrase *Merrily, merrily, merrily, merrily* and an untuned ostinato based on the phrase *Row, row, row your boat.*

1. Learn the song using track 17.

> **Row, row, row your boat,**
> **gently down the stream.**
> **Merrily, merrily, merrily, merrily**
> **life is but a dream.**

2. Teach the action pattern based on the phrase *Merrily, merrily, merrily, merrily.* Repeat using track 18.

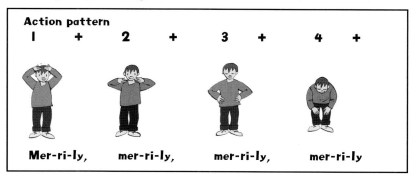

Action pattern							
1	+	2	+	3	+	4	+
Mer-ri-ly,		mer-ri-ly,		mer-ri-ly,		mer-ri-ly	

Divide the class into two groups; one sings the song while the other repeats the action pattern throughout. Swap groups and repeat until everyone has performed both parts.

3. Learn the tuned ostinato part (below) using track 18 and the CD ROM performance activity.

Tuned ostinato pattern							
1	+	2	+	3	+	4	+
C'		G		E		C	
Mer-ri-ly,		mer-ri-ly,		mer-ri-ly,		mer-ri-ly	
Row		row		row	your	boat	

Divide the class into groups again and perform with the different parts, this time replacing the action pattern group with one playing the tuned percussion ostinato pattern.

4. Practise the song with another small group playing the untuned ostinato throughout (below).

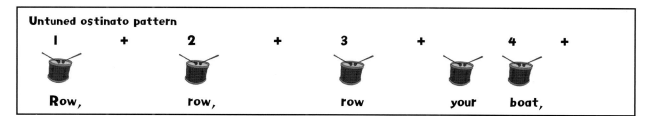

Untuned ostinato pattern							
1	+	2	+	3	+	4	+
Row,		row,		row		your	boat,

5. Divide the children into three groups: one to sing, one to play the tuned percussion ostinato and one to play the untuned percussion ostinato. Perform with the backing track (track 20) and use printouts (CD ROM).

A sailor went to sea

The children play a tuned percussion ostinato and a chord pattern to accompany the song *A sailor went to sea*.

1. Learn the song using track 21.

> A sailor went to sea, sea, sea,
>
> to see what he could see, see, see,
>
> but all that he could see, see, see,
>
> was the bottom of the deep blue sea, sea, sea.

2. Learn the action patten below. Repeat until confident.

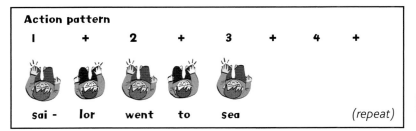

Action pattern								
I	+	2	+	3	+	4	+	
sai -	lor	went	to	sea				*(repeat)*

Divide the class into two groups; one sings the song while the other repeats the action pattern throughout. Swap groups and repeat so that everyone has a chance to try both parts.

3. Learn the tuned ostinato part using track 22 and the CD ROM activity.

Tuned ostinato pattern								
I	+	2	+	3	+	4	+	
A,	A	A,	A					
sai-	lor	went	to	sea				*(repeat)*

A group of children play the ostinato throughout while the others sing the song.

4. Add the chord part by asking the children to choose any of the notes **D**, **F#** and **A** and play them along with the words sea or see eg,

Untuned ostinato pattern								
I	+	2	+	3	+	4	+
				A	A	A	
				F#	F#	F#	
				D	D	D	
sai-lor		went	to	sea,	sea,	sea	

5. Divide the class into three groups: one to sing, one to play the tuned ostinato and one to play the chord part. Perform using track 23 and the printouts.

Swing low

What you will need

 24-27)))   WB

- tuned percussion instruments (eg, xylophones) with these notes for the tuned ostinato part:

  C D F

- some untuned percussion instruments. eg tambourines, woodblocks, maracas.

- CD ROM activity and printout - *Swing low*.

Teachers Tip

The whole class should perform the action pattern with track 24 as many times as necessary for them to be aware that the last line changes. That way, they will be ready when tuned percussion is introduced to change the notes in the last line.

The children play one tuned percussion ostinato pattern and one untuned ostinato pattern to play along with the song *Swing Low*.

1. Learn the song *Swing low* using track 24.

> **Swing low sweet chariot,**
>
> **coming for to carry me home.**
>
> **Swing low, sweet chariot,**
>
> **coming for to carry me home.**

Learn the action pattern. The children repeat the action pattern seven times as they say the words.

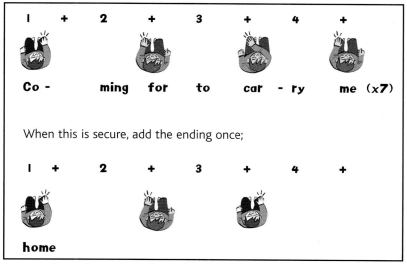

When this is secure, add the ending once;

Complete the action pattern by combining the two sections; the first part seven times and the second part once.

2. Once this is secure, divide the children into two groups; one group sings the song while the other performs the action pattern.

3. Learn the tuned ostinato pattern using track 25 and substituting the actions for notes. Use the CD ROM interactive activity.

1	+	2	+	3	+	4	+
F		C		D		C	
Co -		ming	for	to	car	- ry	me	(x7)
F		C		F			
home							

4. Ask a small group of volunteers to play the complete tuned ostinato while the rest of the class sing the song

5. Another group of children can play the rhythm of the words *Swing low, sweet* throughout. Add this to the song to create a full performance piece. Use printouts (on the CD ROM).

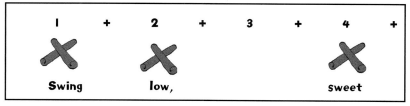

Mango walk

The children learn to play a tuned ostinato and an untuned ostinato along to *Mango walk*.

1. Learn the song using track 28.

> **My brother did-a tell me that you go mango walk,**
>
> **You go mango walk, you go mango walk,**
>
> **My brother did-a tell me that you go mango walk,**
>
> **and steal all the number 'leven.**

2. Teach the action pattern and repeat until secure. The first line must be performed three times followed once by the last line.

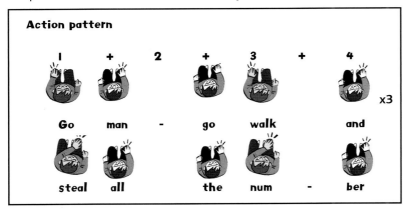

When the children are confident with the actions, divide them into two groups; one to sing the song while the others perform the action pattern.

3. Invite a small group to play the tuned ostinato, *Go mango walk, and steal all the number* (see below), making sure that their hands follow the same directions as the action pattern (ie **D'** will always be played using the right hand).

Tuned ostinato pattern

1	+	2	+	3	+	4
D	D'		D'	D		D'
Go	man -		go	walk		and
D	D'		D'	G		D
steal	all		the	num -		ber

4. Invite a small group to play the word-rhythm that fits with the word *leven (below)*. Encourage the rest of the class to clap the beat softly to help them.

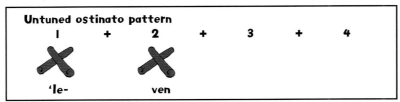

5. Divide the class into three groups: one to sing, one to play the tuned ostinato and one to play the untuned ostinato. Perform using track 30 and printouts (on the CD ROM).

What you will need

28-30

WB

- tuned percussion instruments (eg, xylophones) with these notes for the tuned ostinato part:

  D D'

- some untuned percussion instruments. eg tambourines, woodblocks, maracas.

- CD ROM activity and printout - *Mango walk.*

Teaching tip

Notice that although the song begins after three beats, the actions begin after four beats.

Sarasponda

What you will need

 31-33 WB

- tuned percussion instruments (eg, xylophones) with these notes for the tuned ostinato part:

  ### C' G C

- tuned percussion instruments (eg, xylophones) with these notes for the chord pattern:

  ### C E G

- some untuned percussion instruments. eg tambourines, woodblocks, maracas.

- CD ROM activity and printout - *Sarasponda*.

Teaching Tip
Encourage everyone to sing their parts as they play them.

The children learn the song *Sarasponda* and play a tuned and untuned ostinato to acconpany it. Sarasponda also has a chord pattern which fits with the lyrics *ret set set*.

1. Learn the song using track 31.

> **Sarasponda, sarasponda, sarasponda, ret, set, set**
>
> **Sarasponda, sarasponda, sarasponda, ret, set, set**
>
> **Adorayoh! Adoray boomday-oh!**
>
> **Adoray boomday ret, set, set,**
>
> **Asay, pahsay, oh.**

2. Clap in time to the song. Teach the tuned ostinato part which is played in time with the claps. Use the CD ROM activity to help.

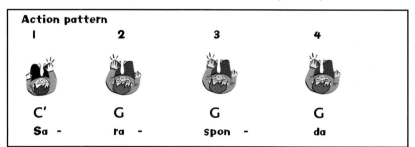

Action pattern			
I	2	3	4
C'	G	G	G
Sa -	ra -	spon -	da

Invite the class to perform the actions while singing the song through. If necessary, use track 31 to help keep in time.

The children play **C'** with the right hand and **G** with the left hand.

Ask a few volunteers to play the tuned ostinato while the rest of the class sing the song.

3. All clap and say the chord pattern *ret set set* along with track 32.

Chord pattern					
I	2		3	4	
G	G	G	G	G	G
E	E	E	E	E	E
C	C	C	C	C	C
Ret,	set,	set	ret,	set,	set

The chord played is three notes **C E G**. Each child picks one of the three notes and plays it to the the rhythm - *ret, set, set.*

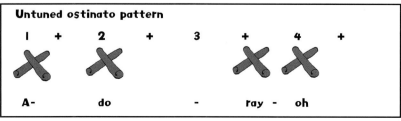

Untuned ostinato pattern							
I	+	2	+	3	+	4	+
A-		do		-		ray -	oh

4. Divide the class into groups and perform the song with all parts. Use the backing track (track 33) and printouts.

Chord accompaniments

Chords and chord accompaniments

Two or more notes played at the same time make a chord. In this section, the children play chord accompaniments by performing three different notes simultaneously with a song.

Counting the beat

Each song has a steady beat which the children must be aware of in order to perform the chord accompaniments. Divide the children into two groups, one to sing the song and the other to count the beat (eg, 1, 2, 3, 4) and clap. This allows the class to hear how the count fits with the song.

Preparing to play a chord accompaniment

It is difficult to sing and play an instrumental part at the same time, so divide the children into singers and players, and then swap roles. The instructions in this section take you and your class through simple preparation leading to a successful performance at the end. It is important to remember that a steady pulse needs to be maintained throughout the song.

Learning a chord accompaniment

The chords are shown in the printouts and on the whiteboard like this:

D'		B
A		G
F		E

The notes are divided among the performers to make the chords easier to play, with one group playing only the high notes at the top, one playing the middle notes and one playing the lower notes at the bottom. This means that each performer will only play a single note at a time. Each part can then be combined to create a chord with all three groups playing their different note at the same time.

Teaching tip

Like the ostinato patterns, the chord patterns in *Percussion Players* are first taught using action patterns. This means that the children must first clap the strong beat of the rhythm until they are confident enough to replace the handclaps with notes and add their instruments.

It is important to remember that when playing the chords, some children play the top note, some play the middle note and some play the bottom note. One child should not play all three notes of the chord, but collectively as a group, the class plays all three notes. The children must try to strike their notes at the same time to create the chords.

What shall we play?

What you will need

 34-35 WB

- Printout (CD ROM).
- CD ROM activity - *What shall we play?*

- These notes for the high part:

  G A

- These notes for the middle part:

  E F

- These notes for the low part:

  C D

- Some untuned percussion instruments (optional).

Teaching Tip
At each of these stages, everyone should lift their hands on the second beat to make sure there is no sound in the gaps.

What shall we play? is sung to the tune of *What shall we do with the drunken sailor?* The children play a three-part chord accompaniment. The chords are played with the pulse of the music on the 'strong' beat.

1. Learn the song using track 34 or whiteboard activity 12.

> **What shall we play in our music lesson?**
> **What shall we play in our music lesson?**
> **What shall we play in our music lesson?**
> **Glockenspiels and chime bars.**
>
> **Drums, tambourines and woodblocks,**
> **Drums, tambourines and woodblocks,**
> **Drums, tambourines and woodblocks,**
> **Glockenspiels and chime bars.**

2. Divide the children into two groups. One group sings the song while the other shows the pulse by clapping only on the first beat and moving hands apart on the second (see below).

Clap the beat

| 1 | 2 | 1 | 2 |

What shall we   play   in our   mu - sic   les - son

3. Make sure that everyone can see a copy of the printout or can see the whiteboard.

While listening to the recording, read one line at a time, pointing to each chord in the appropriate place.

Listen to the recording again (track 34), this time lightly touching the note bars at the correct time.

Divide the class into groups of three and allocate each member of the group a high, middle or low part. Give each group enough time to learn their notes and then play together as a whole class.

4. Choose two or three groups to accompany the class with the chords, while the rest of the class sing. Perform to the backing track on the audio CD.

★ Extend the activity

As a variation you could add some extra instruments to your performance. Choose volunteers to play untuned percussion instruments (eg, tambourines, bells) on the first beats (at the same time as the chords) throughout the song.

John Brown's brother

John Brown's brother is sung to the tune of *John Brown's body*. The children learn to accompany the song using three-note chords. The chords are played with the pulse of the music on the 'strong' beat.

1. Learn the song using track 36 or whiteboard activity 13.

> John Brown's brother ran from here to Timbuktu,
>
> John Brown's brother ran from here to Timbuktu,
>
> John Brown's brother ran from here to Timbuktu,
>
> He's the fastest man alive!
>
>
> Running round the earth's equator,
>
> Rang to say he'd be home later,
>
> What a speedy operator,
>
> He's the fastest man alive!

2. Divide the children into two groups. One group sings while the other shows the pulse by clapping on the first beat and moving hands apart on the second.

Clap the beat

1	2	1	2
John	Brown's	bro -ther	ran from

3. Make sure that everyone can see a copy of the printout or the whiteboard.

While listening to the recording, read one line at a time, pointing to each chord in the appropriate place.

Listen to the recording again, this time lightly touching the note bars at the correct time.

Divide the class into groups of three and allocate each member of the group a high, middle or low part. Give each group enough time to learn their notes and then play together as a whole class.

4. Choose two or three groups to accompany the class with the chords, while the rest of the class sing. Perform to the backing track on the audio CD.

★ Extend the activity

Add some extra instruments to your performance. Choose volunteers to play untuned percussion instruments on the first beats (at the same time as the chords) throughout the song.

What you will need

 36-37 WB

- Printout (CD ROM).
- CD ROM activity - *John Brown's brother*.
- These notes for the high part:

  B C' D'
- These notes for the middle part:

  G A
- These notes for the low part:

  D E F#

- Some untuned percussion instruments (optional).

Chord accompaniments

My bonnie

What you will need

 38-39 WB

• Printout (CD ROM).

• CD ROM activity - *My bonnie*.

• These notes for the high part:

B C' D'

• These notes for the middle part:

G A

• These notes for the low part:

D E F#

• Some untuned percussion instruments (optional).

Teacher's Tip:
Notice that the tune begins before the 1st beat. This is called an upbeat. 123 My bon-nie lies o-ver the ocean

---

The children learn to accompany the song *My bonnie lies over the ocean* using three-note chords. The chords are played with the pulse of the music on the 'strong' beat of each bar.

1. Learn the song using track 38 or whiteboard activity 14.

> **My bonnie lies over the ocean,**
>
> **My bonnie lies over the sea,**
>
> **My bonnie lies over the ocean,**
>
> **Oh bring back my bonnie to me.**
>
> **Bring back, bring back,**
>
> **Oh, bring back my bonnie to me, to me.**
>
> **Bring back, bring back,**
>
> **Oh, bring back my bonnie to me.**

2. Teach the children the action pattern below. Divide the children into two groups; one group sings while the other shows the pulse by clapping on the first beat and keeping hands apart on the second and third beats (see below).

Clap the beat

(3) | My   1 | bon   2 | - nie   3 | lies   1 | o   2 | - ver   3 | the...

3. Make sure that everyone can see a copy of the printout or the whiteboard.

While listening to the recording, read one line at a time, pointing to each chord in the appropriate place.

Listen to the recording again, this time lightly touching the note bars at the correct time.

Divide the class into groups of three and allocate each member of the group a high, middle or low part. Give each group enough time to learn their notes and then play together as a whole class.

4. Choose two or three groups to accompany the class with the chords, while the rest of the class sing. Perform to the backing track on the audio CD.

★ Extend the activity

Add some extra instruments to your performance. Choose volunteers to play untuned percussion instruments on the first beats (at the same time as the chords) throughout the song.

Simple gifts

The children learn to accompany the song *Simple gifts* using three-note chords. The chords are played with the pulse of the music on the 'strong' beat.

What you will need

 40-41 WB

• Printout (CD ROM).

• CD ROM activity - *Simple gifts*.

• These notes for the high part:
  C' D' E'

• These notes for the middle part:
  A B

• These notes for the low part:
  E F# G

1. Learn the song using track 40 or whiteboard activity 15.

> **'Tis the gift to be simple, 'tis the gift to be free,**
>
> **'Tis the gift to come down where you ought to be,**
>
> **And when we find ourselves in the place just right,**
>
> **'Twill be in the valley of love and delight.**
>
> **When true simplicity is gained,**
>
> **To bow and to bend we shan't be ashamed;**
>
> **To turn, turn will be our delight,**
>
> **'Til by turning, turning we come round right.**

2. Divide the children into two groups. One group sings while the other counts the beats throughout clapping on the first and third beats.

3. Make sure that everyone can see a copy of the printout or whiteboard.

While listening to the recording, read one line at a time, pointing to each chord in the appropriate place.

Listen to the recording again, this time lightly touching the note bars at the correct time.

Divide the class into groups of three and allocate each member of the group a high, middle or low part. Give each group enough time to learn their notes and then play together as a class.

4. Choose two or three groups to accompany the class with the chords, while the rest of the class sing. Perform to track 41 (backing only).

★ Extend the activity

Add some extra instruments to your performance. Choose volunteers to play untuned percussion instruments on the first beats (at the same time as the chords) throughout the song.

Teaching tip

Notice that the tune begins on the beat before the 1st beat. This is called the upbeat.

(4)	1	2	3	4
'Tis the gift	to	be	sim-ple	tis the

Chord accompaniments

Daisy bell

What you will need

 42-43 WB

• Printout (CD ROM).

• CD ROM activity - *Daisy bell.*

• These notes for the high part:

  C' D' E'

• These notes for the middle part:

  A Bb B C'

• These notes for the low part:

  F G

The children learn to accompany the song *Daisy bell* using three-note chords. The chords are played with the pulse of the music on the 'strong'; beat.

1. Learn the song using track 42 or whiteboard activity 16.

   Daisy, Daisy,

   Give me your answer, do!

   I'm half crazy,

   All for the love of you!

   It won't be a stylish marriage,

   I can't afford a carriage,

   But you'll look sweet upon the seat

   Of a bicycle made for two!

2. Divide the children into two groups; one sings while the other counts the beat throughout, clapping on the first beats.

3. Make sure that everyone can see a copy of the printout or whiteboard.

   While listening to the recording, read one line at a time, pointing to each chord in the appropriate place.

   Listen to the recording again, this time lightly touching the note bars at the correct time.

   Divide the class into groups of three and allocate each member of the group a high, middle or low part. Give each group enough time to learn their chords and then try practising them as a whole class.

4. Choose two or three groups to accompany the class with the chords, while the rest of the class sing. Perform to the backing track on the audio CD.

★ Extend the activity

Add some extra instruments to your performance. Choose volunteers to play untuned percussion instruments on the first beats (at the same time as the chords) throughout the song.

Pokarekare ana

The children learn to accompany the song *Pokarekare ana* using three-note chords. The chords are played with the pulse of the music on the 'strong' beat.

1. Learn the song using track 44 or whiteboard activity 17.

> **Pokarekare ana**
>
> **Ngā wai o Waiapu**
>
> **Whiti atu koe hine**
>
> **Marinoana e**
>
> **E hine e**
>
> **Hoki mai ra**
>
> **Ka mate ahau**
>
> **I te aroha e**

2. Listen to the song again, this time clapping on the first and third beats.

Clap the beat

| 1 | 2 | 3 | 4 | 1 | 2 | 3 | 4 |

Po - ka-re- ka-re a - na

3. Make sure that everyone can see a copy of the printout or the whiteboard.

While listening to the recording, read one line at a time, pointing to each chord in the appropriate place.

Listen to the recording again, this time lightly touching the note bars at the correct time.

Divide the class into groups of three and allocate each member of the group a high, middle or low part. Give each group enough time to learn their notes and then play together as a class.

4. Choose two or three groups to accompany the class with the chords, while the rest of the class sing. Use the backing track on the audio CD.

★ Extend the activity

Add some extra instruments to your performance. Choose volunteers to play untuned percussion instruments on the first beats (at the same time as the chords) throughout the song.

What you will need

 44-46)))   WB

• Printout (CD ROM)

• CD ROM activity - *Pokarekare ana*.

• These notes for the high part:
  D' E'
• These notes for the middle part:
  A B C
• These notes for the low part:
  F# G

Teacher's Tip

Notice that although the chords begin on the first beat, the tune and singing begins on the 2nd beat.

1 + 2 + 3 + 4 +

Po- ka-re-ka-re

Teacher's Tip

To help with the pronunciation of the lyrics, use track 45. First listen, and then sing back the phrases one-by-one. This is called 'echo-singing' and is an effective way to learn songs.

Greensleeves

What you will need

 47-48))) WB

• Printout (CD ROM)

• CD ROM activity - *Greensleeves*.

• These notes for the high part:

  B' D'

• These notes for the middle part:

  G A B

• These notes for the low part:

  E F# G

Teacher's Tip

Notice that the tune begins on beat 6 (before beat 1).

1 2 3 4 5 6   1 2 3 4 5 6

         A- las, my love you

The children learn to accompany the song *Greensleeves* using three-note chords. The beats are in groups of six and each chord is played on the first and fourth beats. This is still the 'strong' beat of the bar. Clapping in time will help the children learn when to play their notes (see below).

I. Learn the song using track 47 or whiteboard activity 18.

> Alas, my love, you do me wrong,
>
> To cast me off discourteously;
>
> And I have loved you for so long,
>
> Delighting in your company.
>
> Greensleeves was all my joy,
>
> Greensleeves was my delight,
>
> Greensleeves was my heart of gold
>
> And who but my Lady Greensleeves?

Divide the children into two groups; one sings while the other counts the beats, clapping on the 1st and 4th beats.

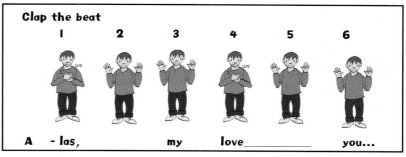

Clap the beat

| I | 2 | 3 | 4 | 5 | 6 |

A - las,   my   love_____   you...

2. Make sure that everyone can see a copy of the printout or whiteboard.

While listening to the recording, read one line at a time, pointing to each chord in the appropriate place.

Listen to the recording again, this time lightly touching the note bars at the correct time.

Divide the class into groups of three and allocate each member of the group a high, middle or low part. Give each group enough time to learn their notes and then play them together as a whole class.

3. Choose two or three groups to accompany the class with the chords, while the rest of the class sing. Use printouts and the backing track on the audio CD for a full performance.

★ Extend the activity

Add some extra instruments to your performance. Choose volunteers to play untuned percussion instruments on the first beats (at the same time as the chords) throughout the song.

Sambalele

The children learn the song *Sambalele* and accompany it using chords, a tuned ostinato and untuned ostinato. You will notice that *Sambalele* has more parts and complex rhythms than other songs in the book. Use the tracks and whiteboard activity as a warm-up and to learn the songs thoroughly before the full performance.

I. Learn the song using track 49 or whiteboard activity 19.

> **Sambalele is a monkey,**
>
> **When he is dancing he's funky.**
>
> **He likes the way he is moving**
>
> **Friends say there's room for improving.**
>
> **Samba, samba, sambó lêlê**
>
> **Samba, samba, sambó lálá**
>
> **Samba, samba, sambó lêlê**
>
> **Na barra da saia ó lálá**

Untuned ostinato accompaniment

I. Find the pulse in the song Sambalele

Listen to the recording of the song *Sambalele* (track 49). Ask the class to step to the beat. To find the pulse they should step on the first and the third beats (see illustrations below).

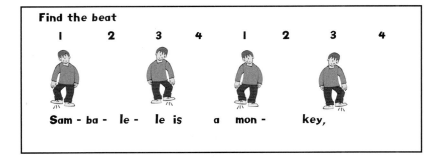

Find the beat

2. Play the beat using the instruments

Accompany the song by using untuned percussion instruments to play on the beats while the rest of the class sing the song (if they feel confident, they can continue to step to the beat). Use track 50.

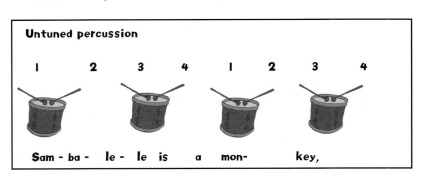

Untuned percussion

What you will need

- Printout (CD ROM).

- CD ROM activity - *Sambalele*.

- This note for the 1st part
  G
- This note for the 2nd part
  E F
- This note for the 3rd part
  B, C
- These notes for the tuned ostinato
  G G'

- Some untuned percussion instruments.

Sambalele

What you will need

- Printout (CD ROM).

- CD ROM activity - *Sambalele*.

- This note for the 1st part

  G

- This note for the 2nd part

  E F

- This note for the 3rd part

  B, C

- These notes for the tuned ostinato

  G G'

- Some untuned percussion instruments.

4. Add an untuned ostinato to the pulse

Choose a bell-like untuned instrument (eg cowbell, agogo bell) and add a samba-style rhythm to the accompaniment. Use track 51 to help. Use track 51 and the illustrations below to help learn this more complex rhythm. Accompany the song with both untuned parts.

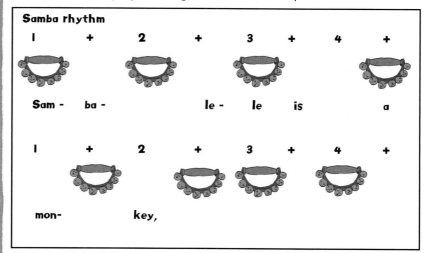

Tuned ostinato accompaniment

5. Listen to track 51- the tuned ostinato.

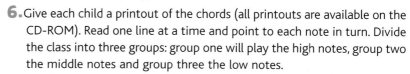

Practise the tuned ostinato accompaniment together. Play along with track 51 to help keep in time.

Chord accompaniment

6. Give each child a printout of the chords (all printouts are available on the CD-ROM). Read one line at a time and point to each note in turn. Divide the class into three groups: group one will play the high notes, group two the middle notes and group three the low notes.

Listen to track 51and lightly touch the note bars on the pulse (beats 1 and 3).

When confident create a full performance piece by combining the chord part with singers and playing to the backing track (track 52).

Discuss how to perform the song. Decide who will play which accompaniment parts and choose a variety of instruments. The class play the tuned accompaniment or chord pattern, and some play rhythms on untuned percussion instruments. To add interest the singers may wish to clap or stamp the pulse as they sing. Make full use of the whiteboard activity, the printouts and the audio CD to create a successful performance.

Learning tunes

This section contains melodies for tuned percussion instruments that can be used for performances or class assemblies. All of the songs can be played along with the CD backing tracks and some also have an added ostinato and/or second parts for more able pupils.

All of the parts are available on the CD ROM and and can be photocopied for use in the classroom.

There are opportunities for singing as well as playing melody lines. Performances can be tailored to suit your available resources and the varying abilities within your class.

When learning a new tune, it is often helpful to divide up the phrases and learn each section separately before putting the whole thing together to create a finished performance piece.

Melody:

• Melody is another name for the tune or main part in a piece of music.

Accompaniment:

• Accompaniment is the word used to describe music that is used in the background to support the melody or main tune.

Questions you might ask

Do the notes always move around or do they sometimes stay the same?

If they move, do they go up or down?

Do the notes move in small steps or in big leaps?

Get interactive

Every song in *Percussion Players* has an interactive performance activity on the CD ROM. This enables the class to watch the lyrics of the song and the notes in the melody and play along. Each activity has a printout of the tune part for the children to follow. Printouts are available on the CD ROM.

You can print the song melodies and give them to the class so that they can play along with the interactive activity.

The interactive songs are often a shortened version of the song on the CD. This is so that the children can practise their tunes, warm up and then use the printouts for a full performance with the entire class including untuned instruments.

Teaching tip

Like the ostinato patterns, tunes to play in *Percussion Players* are first taught using actions. Rather than clapping the children mark out the pitch of the tune by moving their arms up or down according to whether the note has moved lower or higher. This will help to understand the movement of the tune until the children are confident enough to add their own instruments.

It is important that the children understand that their melody on the instruments is the same as the singing part. Therefore, in group performance urge them to practise initially with the singers alone.

Suo-gân

What you will need

 53-54

- some tuned percussion instruments with these notes:

  G A B

- Printout (CD ROM)
- CD ROM activity - *Suo-gân*.
- some untuned percussion instruments.

1. Teach the song *Suo-gân* using track 53 and whiteboard activity 21.

   Suo-gân do not weep
   Suo-gân go to sleep

2. Listen to the song again. With the class, follow the pitch movement of the melody by raising and lowering your hands to match. It may be necessary to repeat this a few times to ensure that everyone has become familiar with the tune.

3. Give each group a set of chime bar notes or another tuned instrument with **G A B**.

   Tell the class that the tune begins with the note **G**. They must use the instruments to work out the tune.

4. When you have found the correct order, invite several children to play it along with the backing track (track 54) while the rest of the class sing. Add untuned percussion for a full performance. Printouts can be found on the CD ROM.

Land of the silver birch

What you will need

 53-54

- some tuned instruments with these notes

  D F G A C' D'

- some untuned percussion instruments.
- Printout (CD ROM).
- CD ROM activity - *Land of the silver birch*.

1. Teach the song *Land of the silver birch* using track 55 and whiteboard activity 21.

   Land of the silver birch,
   Home of the beaver,
   Where still the mighty moose wanders at will.
   Blue lake and rocky shore,
   I will return once more.
   Boom didi a da
   Boom didi a da
   Boom didi a da
   Boom.

2. Listen to the song again. With the class, follow the pitch movement of the melody by raising and lowering your hands to match (eg, when the note gets higher the arm raises, and vice versa). Repeat this step as many times as is necessary until all members of the class are able to show the pitch correctly.

3. Give each group a set of chime bar notes and ask the children to put the notes into the correct order for each phrase (line) of the song.

   Ask volunteers to help you to arrange the notes into the correct order.

4. When you have found the correct order, invite several children to play along with the backing track while the rest of the class sing. Add untuned percussion or create chord accompaniments or ostinati for a full performance. Printouts can be downloaded from the CD ROM.

Tunes to play

When the saints

1. Teach the song *When the saints* using track 59 and whiteboard activity 23.

> Oh when the saints go marching in,
> Oh when the saints go marching in
> I want to be in that number,
> When the saints go marching in.

2. Listen to the song again. With the class, follow the pitch movement of the melody by raising and lowering your hands to match. Repeat this step as many times as is necessary until all members of the class are able to show the pitch correctly (remember, when the note gets higher, the arm raises, and vice versa).

3. Use the the notes **GABCD'** to work out the melody without using the printout or whiteboard.

4. When everybody has worked out the melody, choose individuals to play it while the rest of the class sing. Perform to the backing track and use printouts from the CD ROM.

What you will need

53-54

WB

- some tuned instruments with these notes:
  G A B C' D'

- some untuned percussion instruments.

- Printout (CD ROM).

- CD ROM activity - *When the saints.*

All the pretty horses

1. Teach the song *All the pretty horses* using track 61 and whiteboard activity 24.

> Hushaby, don't you cry,
> Go to sleepy little baby.
> When you wake you shall have,
> All the pretty little horses.
> Blacks and Bays, Dapples and Grays,
> Coach and six-a little horses.
> Hushaby, don't you cry,
> Go to sleepy little baby.

Listen to the song again. With the class follow the pitch movement of the melody by raising and lowering your hands to match. It may be necessary to repeat this a few times to ensure that everyone has become familiar with the tune.

2. Listen to the song and work out together how many different musical phrases are in it (four - some phrases are repeated). Divide the class into groups to each play one phrase or swap phrases.

3. Give each child the printout (from the CD ROM) and instruments with the correct notes on.

Using the printout slowly learn the melody until confident.

4. Perform *All the pretty horses* as a class. Divide the class into groups of singers and players.

What you will need

61-62

WB

- These tuned percussion notes:
  A, C, D E F G A Bb C

- some untuned percussion instruments.

- Printout (CD ROM).

- CD ROM activity - *All the pretty horses.*

Tunes to play

Migldi magldi

What you will need

 63-64 WB

- some tuned instruments with these notes:

A, B, C D E F G A B C' D' E'

- some untuned percussion instruments.
- Printout (CD ROM).
- CD ROM activity - *Migldi Magldi*.

1. Teach the song *Migldi magldi* using track 63 or whiteboard activity 25. Sing together.

> **What a funny sight to see,**
> **Migldi magldi, hey now now!**
> **A wide open door for me,**
> **Migldi Magldi, hey now now!**
> **There's the blacksmith working hard**
> **Migldi magldi, hey now now,**
> **And his dog is standing guard**
> **Migldi magldi, hey now now!**

2. Listen to the song again. With the class, follow the pitch movement of the melody by raising and lowering your hands to match. It may be necessary to repeat this a few times to ensure that everyone has become familiar with the tune.

3. As a class work out the different phrases or sections in this song. Once confident, divide the class into small groups and give each half a number - 1 or 2. The groups can play a phrase/line each (taking turns like a call and response).

4. When you have found the correct order, invite several children to play along with the backing track while the rest of the class sing. Use the printouts (CD ROM), the interactive activity and the audio CD to learn the parts.

★ Extend the activity

- Give five volunteers a phrase each. See if they can perform the song by playing their phrase in the correct place.

Tunes to play

Composing

Discussing composition

Before asking the children to compose, consider and discuss with them the tools with which professional composers make their music interesting and effective. These are called the musical elements (see glossary).

Musical elements

These are the components that make up any piece of music. They are: pitch, duration, dynamics, tempo, timbre, texture and structure. See glossary at the back of the book for definitions.

Composing activities

Each activity in this section consists of a simple process for the children to go through in order to create their own music. Be aware that when composing music, there are no wrong or right ideas, though some may be more effective or appropriate than others.

Performance and appraisal

First and foremost, encourage the children to enjoy their music-making and to develop the means and confidence to perform independently of your help. When they are performing, encourage the children to:

- be ready to play;
- begin together at an agreed signal or count in;
- listen carefully to one other.

When appraising class performances, it is important to commend them not only on content, but also on presentation and organisation as well.

Encourage the children to evaluate their own performances. They should actively try to consider how they aim to achieve a musical effect and look for ways to improve on it. A simple way of doing this is to record each performance and then play it back to the class, encouraging them to ask the following questions such as:

What did you like most in the music?

How do you think it could be improved?

Describe the mood of the music? What does it remind you of?

Get interactive

The interactive whiteboard is an extremely effective aid for composition in the classroom. The *Percussion Players* CD-ROM contains composition activities which compliment the activities in this chapter.

Mostly the interactive activities contain full colour versions of the pictures in this chapter which the children must compose to.

It is a great idea to project the pictures onto the screen in full view of the children so that you can discuss possible composition techniques together.

Also, when the children divide into groups for individual composition activities, the interactive activities can be viewed on individual screens by each group and worked to.

For those activities which involve composing to a storyboard, the interactive whiteboard allows you or the children to flick back and forth between images easily.

Tools for composition

Consider and discuss the tools with which professional composers make their music interesting and effective.

using the musical elements - pitch, duration, dynamics, tempos, timbre, texture and structure;
mood and feel (all the elements);
melody or tune (pitch);
chords - more than one notes at a time (pitch),
repetition, contrast and the construction and shape of a piece (structure).

Composing

Playing pictures

What you will need:

WB

- as many tuned and untuned instruments as you have available.
- As varied a collection of pictures from as wide a range of sources as you like (you may photocopy pictures from this page).
- a recording device.
- as many tuned and untuned instruments as you have available.
- CD ROM activity - *Playing pictures*.

The children compose music using ideas suggested by a picture. They are then encouraged to think about the different musical elements used to create a piece.

1. Divide the children into small groups. Each group chooses, or is allocated, a picture from the CD ROM or one collected in class.

2. The children find sounds suggested by their picture.

   Sounds can be suggested by any aspect of a picture:

   - the subject, features or background;
   - style (and colours);
   - a suggested event;
   - mood.

   Some pictures may suggest obvious sounds, whereas others may require more imagination. Encourage the children to think about what their music can represent e.g. twinkling stars, rather than just sound effects.

3. The children explore three ways to organise their sounds into compositions.

   Each group tries all of the following approaches:

   - To cue sounds, a conductor might point one by one to elements on the picture that suggest sounds.
   - To cue the beginning and ends of sounds, a conductor can move a ruler vertically from left to right across the picture.
   - Sounds can be ordered according to an agreed sequence of events suggested by the picture.

4. Each group evaluates and compares its resulting compositions. Ask each group to perform their piece and record the results. At the end, listen to the recording of each composition and hold a class discussion about it.

Composing

A musical sandwich

What you will need

65)))

• Instruments with the notes of the C pentatonic scale.

C, D E G A

• CD ROM activity - *A musical sandwich*.

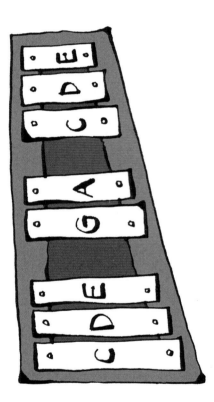

In groups, the children make up a short piece using just two musical phrases: **A** and **B**. The phrases are organised into the structure A B A and can be combined to create a more substantial class piece

1. Choose a subject, such as food, articles of clothing, famous personalities, schoolwork-related ideas, and so on, for which the children can think of two phrases.

2. Divide the class into small groups of four or five.

Each group thinks of two different phrases and labels one phrase A and the other phrase B.

Both of the phrases should be of a similar length and have contrasting rhythms. eg

A	**Wellington boots,**
B	**Muddy puddle,**
A	**Wellington boots.**

A	**London, Paris, Washington, Rome,**
B	**Capital cities of the world,**
A	**London, Paris, Washington, Rome.**

A	**Six sevens are forty-two,**
B	**Ten nines are ninety,**
A	**Six sevens are forty-two.**

A	**Yellow and blue,**
B	**Together they're green,**
A	**Yellow and blue.**

3. Each pair then turn their phrases into a poem by using the structure ABA.

Encourage the children to perform their poems to the rest of the class.

4. The children then compose a melody line for their poem. The tunes should fit the rhythms of the invented phrases (one note for each syllable).

Encourage the children to use all available notes or to repeat notes or play more than one at a time. The tunes can either be memorised or written down.

5. The children play their musical phrases in the A B A structure to make a piece of music. Give them the opportunity to perform the pieces to the other children. Discuss the compositions together.

★ Extend the activity

Join all the groups' pieces together to create a whole class composition. Record a performance of it and then listen back to it together. Discuss favourite parts and how it could be improved.

• Try the following structures; AABA

• Add a new C section; ABACA (rondo form) or ABCBA (arch form)

Secrets of the animal kingdom

What you will need

 66)))

- at least two instruments with the notes of the same pentatonic scale.

- The instrument below shows the notes of the pentatonic scale of G.

  G A B D' E'

- The pentatonic scale of F is

  F G A C' D'

- The pentatonic scale of C is

  C D E G A

The children make up a call and response piece. The call should be different each time, but the response is always the same.

1. Introduce the idea of a call and response structure to the class.

   Listen to the call and response on the recording (track 66).

Call:	**How many spots on a spotty dalmation?**
Response:	*Secrets of the animal kingdom.*
Call:	**How much does a kingfisher weigh?**
Response:	*Secrets of the animal kingdom.*
Call:	**What does a baby armadillo eat?**
Response:	*Secrets of the animal kingdom.*
Call:	**Do whales sleep?**
Response:	*Secrets of the animal kingdom.*

   Choose individual children to perform each call ('How many spots on a spotty dalmation'). The rest of the class reply with the response ('Secrets of the animal kingdom').

   Once the children are confident performing the responses encourage the children to make up different calls using their own questions about the animal kingdom.

2. The children play the word rhythms of the call and response with actions (eg, clapping, knee-tapping). Although the response will be the same every time, each call can be a different sequence of sounds.

   Keep a steady pulse going throughout and try to begin each new call without a break.

3. The children replace the body percussion sounds with tunes or rhythms played on any available instruments. Agree on a fixed rhythm or tune for the response and make up different ones for the call.

4. The children perform their call and response compositions to the class. Some children can say the chant while others play the melody and rhythms on a variety of tuned and untuned percussion instruments.

5. Discuss and evaluate the compositions together. Suggest ways in which they might be improved. If possible record the performance so that the groups can listen to themselves play.

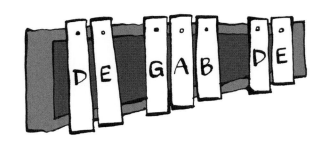

The intrepid traveller

This activity allows the children to create a class composition to illustrate the journey of a traveller, while also exploring mood and feel. Dynamics (loud and quiet sounds) are explored through the changing condition of geographical features – water, a volcano, snow and a tropical storm.

What you will need

 WB

- As many tuned and untuned percussion instruments as you have available.
- CD ROM activity - *The intrepid traveller.*

1. Discuss the changing geographical features encountered in the explorer's journey.

The children can look at pictures of the explorer's journey on the CD ROM. Discuss how:

- the water increases from a stream to an ocean (1-3);
- the volcano goes from calm to angry (3-5);
- the snow falls and gathers (6-8);
- the tropical storm gathers momentum (9-10).

2. The changing geographical features in the explorer's journey can be suggested in music with changing dynamics.

Discuss ways to change dynamics, such as:

- changing the way in which you play an instrument to give a louder or quieter effect;
- increasing or decreasing the number instruments playing together;
- choosing loud or quiet instruments (a large cymbal, played with the same effort as Indian bells, will sound louder);
- any combination of these.

Discuss the musical effect of increasing or decreasing volume in music.

3 Divide the children into four groups and delegate a geographical feature to each (water, volcano). Encourage them to choose appropriate instruments and to use suitable dynamics.

4. The children perform in the order shown in the illustrations without a pause between sections, making one piece of music depicting the explorer's whole journey.

The interactive composition activity for The intrepid traveller on the CD ROM can be used to great effect. The pictures of the explorer's journey appear on screen in order. Each group must be ready to begin their composition as soon as their pcture flashes up. Also try this activity with many different pictures from a variety of sources, all depicting different environments and journeys. The more stimuli the children have to compose to the better.

Composing

Make a note of your birthday

What you will need

- As many tuned and untuned percussion instruments as you can find.
- Photocopies of the birthday code (page 46).
- Paper and pencils.

The children use their dates of birth and the birthday code to make short tunes. These are incorporated and developed into a composition.

1. Each child writes down his or her date of birth in number form, eg 18 08 2000.

2. Give each child a copy of the Birthday code(page 46). Each child uses the birthday code to play their own birthday melody. They can be creative with rhythms and are urged to use any notes with a sharp and a flat for a zero (0).

3. Divide the children into groups. Each group considers how to organise its birthday tunes into a larger composition. The children may:

   - play their tunes one after another to make one long tune;
   - repeat a tune or parts of a tune;
   - play two tunes simultaeously;
   - use contrasting volume (play loudly or quietly);
   - develop accompaniments for their compositions using untuned percussion instruments of their chioice.

4. Each group now plays its composition to the class. Use the prompts at the beginning of this chapter to discuss and evaluate the compositions together. It is a good idea to record the compositions if possible so that the composers can listen to their own work and decide ways in which it could be changed or improved. They may wish to display their plan ,explaining what it shows before performing their compositions. The children should;

   - use a wide variety of tuned and untuned percussion instruments;
   - experiment with different rhythms;
   - try adding a vocal part with lyrics to their composition?
   - Decide how many people will be playing at once - solos, small groups, in unison or as a round?

Composing

Birthday code

1.  C

2. D

3.  E

4. F

5.  G

6. A

7.  B

8. C

9. silent rest

0. any note with a sharp or flat in its name.

Whatever the weather

What you will need

- as many tuned and untuned percussion instruments as you can make available.

First the children can list different kinds of weather and discuss words to describe them. Use pictures or collected items in the classroom as visual stimuli for composition.

1. Divide the children into groups. Each group makes a selection of weather types and, for each, it makes up a short section of music. Allow the children to choose from various instruments in order to create sounds suggested by the various trypes of weather.

2. The short sections of weather music are ordered according to weather sequences. Each group thinks of a weather sequence and orders its short sections of music according to it. Some weather sequences may produce more effective pieces of music than others. Allow the children time to experiment with different weather sequences and to choose the one they feel makes the most effective piece of music.

3. Each group performs a piece of music based on its chosen weather sequence. If you wish, the rest of the class can try to work out the weather sequence of each piece by listening.

4. The groups can write or draw their weather sequences (eg storm cloud, thunder bolt, sunshine). They might want to display their sequence to the class and explain the thinking behind their compositions.

Spelling bee

A sample rondo composition

B A D G E (A section)

E B B (B section)

B A D G E (A section)

C A F E (C section)

B A D G E (A section)

D E C A D E (D section)

B A D G E (A section)

In this activity the children choose melodies made by words spelt with letters that are note names. The children order the melodies according to musical structure called *rondo*. In a rondo the first section (called the A section) is repeated after contrasting sections of music (called the B section, C section and so on), making an A B A C A D A structure. (Remember here the letters are not notes names).

1. Divide the children into groups. Each group finds four words which, when the letters names are played as notes, make pleasing melodies. The words can be any length. (see examples in 'A sample rondo composition')

2. Each group finds ways to perform its melodies - quickly, slowly, with particiular rhythms or with sounds played on other percussion instruments.

3. Each group decides which of its melodies should be the A section, B section and so on in their rondo structured composition. The melody used for the A section should be performed in the same way each time it is repeated. The other sections should contrast with the A section. They might contrast by having:

- a different number of notes in the melody;
- a different starting and end note;
- a different rhythm;
- a different mode of performance or accompaniment.

Example printout - Sambalele

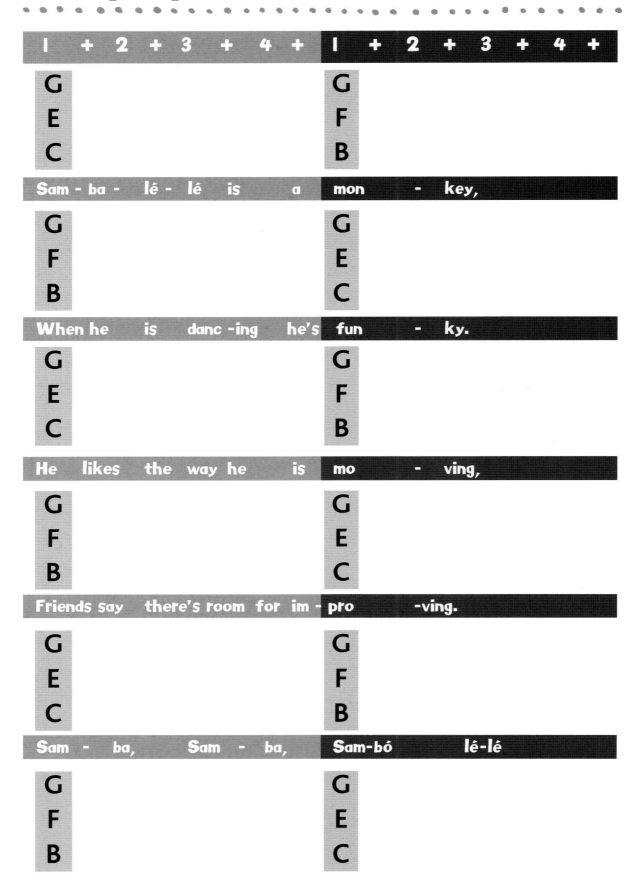

Percussion Players © 2008 A&C Black Publishers Ltd

Example printout - Sambalele 2

1	+	2	+	3	+	4	+	1	+	2	+	3	+	4	+
G E C								G F B							

Sam	-	ba,	Sam	-	ba,	Sam-bó	lé- lé

G F B								G E C							

Na	ba	-	rra	da	Saia	lá- lá

Example printout - Daisy bell

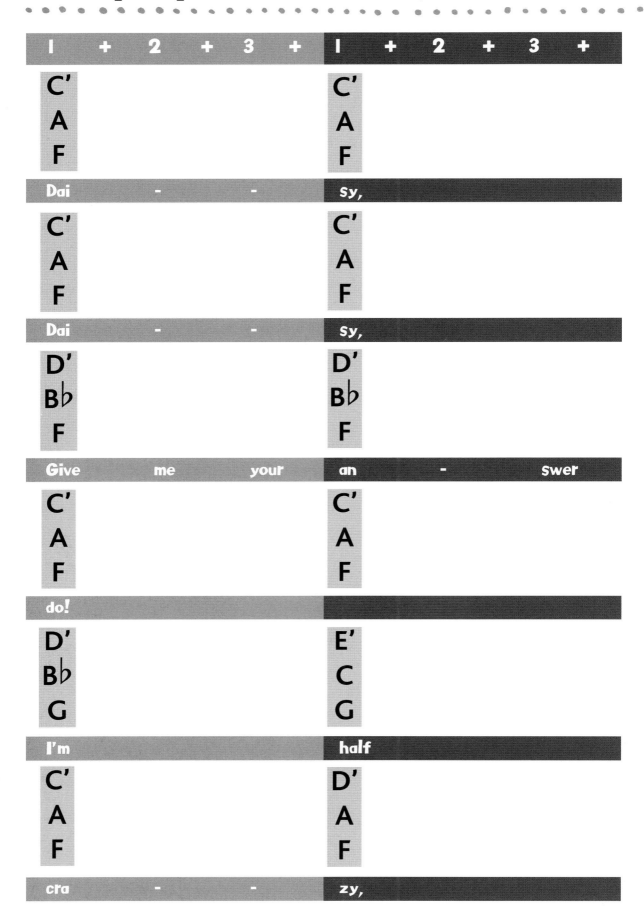

1	+	2	+	3	+	1	+	2	+	3	+
C' A F						C' A F					
Dai		–		–		sy,					
C' A F						C' A F					
Dai		–		–		sy,					
D' B♭ F						D' B♭ F					
Give		me		your		an		–		swer	
C' A F						C' A F					
do!											
D' B♭ G						E' C G					
I'm						half					
C' A F						D' A F					
cra		–		–		zy,					

Example printout - Daisy bell 2

1	+	2	+	3	+	1	+	2	+	3	+
D' B G						D' B G					

| All | | for | | the | | love | | | | of | |

| E' C G | | | | | | E' C G | | | | | |

| you! | | | | | | | | | | It | |

| E' C G | | | | | | E' C G | | | | | |

| won't | | be | | a | | sty | | - | | lish | |

| C' A F | | | | | | C' A F | | | | | |

| mar - riage, | | | | | | | | | | I | |

| D' B♭ F | | | | | | D' B♭ F | | | | | |

| can't | | af | | - | | ford | | | | a | |

| E' C G | | | | | | E' C G | | | | | |

| car - riage, | | | | | | | | | | But | |

Example printout - Daisy bell 3

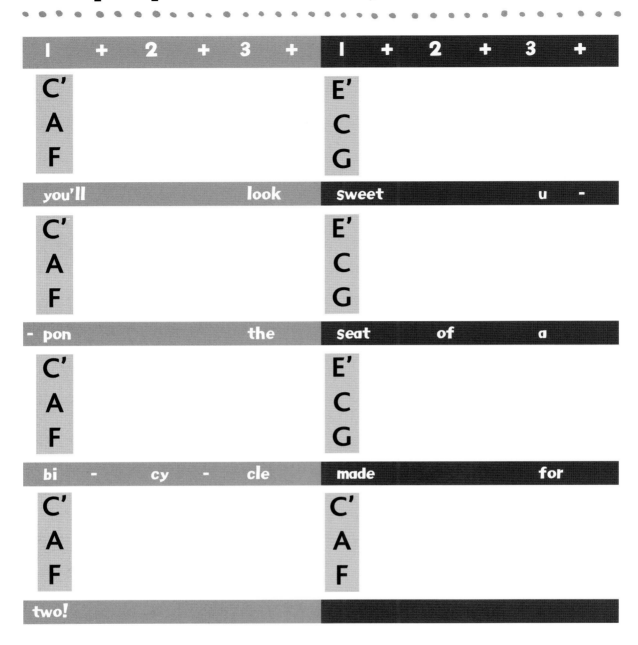

1	+	2	+	3	+	1	+	2	+	3	+
C' A F						E' C G					
you'll				look		sweet				u	-
C' A F						E' C G					
- pon				the		seat		of		a	
C' A F						E' C G					
bi	-	cy	-	cle		made				for	
C' A F						C' A F					
two!											

Example printout - What shall we play?

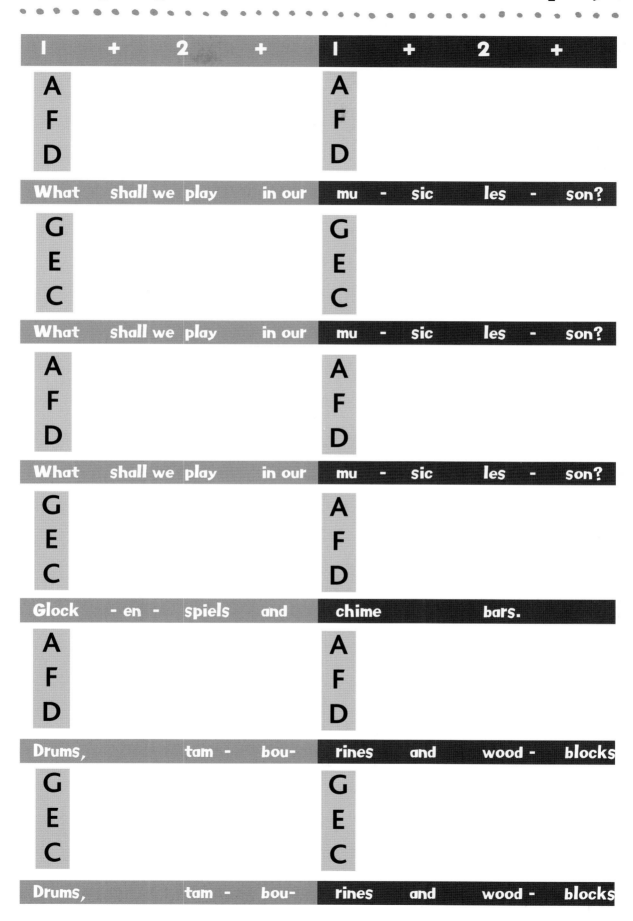

1	+	2	+	1	+	2	+
A F D				A F D			
What	shall we	play	in our	mu -	sic	les -	son?
G E C				G E C			
What	shall we	play	in our	mu -	sic	les -	son?
A F D				A F D			
What	shall we	play	in our	mu -	sic	les -	son?
G E C				A F D			
Glock	- en -	spiels	and	chime		bars.	
A F D				A F D			
Drums,		tam -	bou-	rines	and	wood -	blocks
G E C				G E C			
Drums,		tam -	bou-	rines	and	wood -	blocks

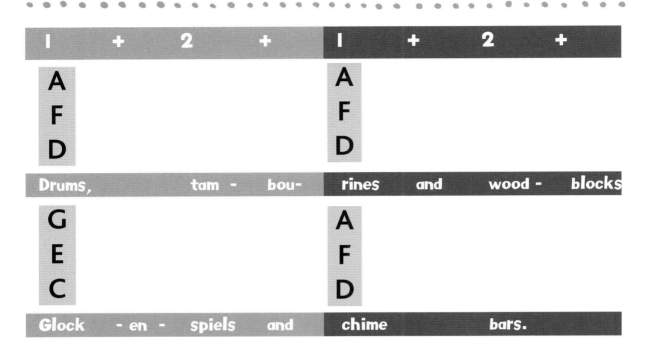

Melody lines

High, low, middle

Which notes are these?

London's burning

Frère Jacques

Melody lines

Row, row, row your boat

Row, row, row your boat, Gen - tly down the stream.

Mer - ri - ly, mer - ri - ly, mer - ri - ly, mer - ri - ly, Life is but a dream.

A sailor went to sea

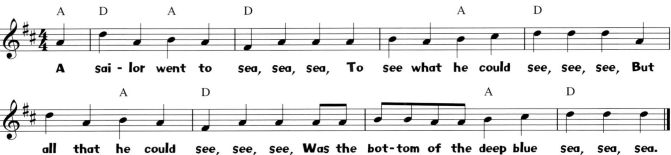

A sai - lor went to sea, sea, sea, To see what he could see, see, see, But

all that he could see, see, see, Was the bot - tom of the deep blue sea, sea, sea.

Swing low, sweet chariot

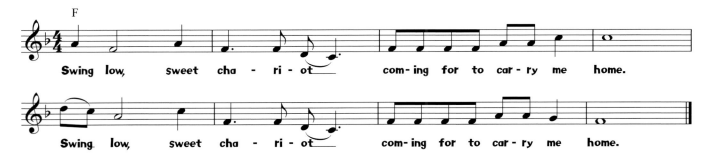

Swing low, sweet cha - ri - ot com - ing for to car - ry me home.

Swing low, sweet cha - ri - ot com - ing for to car - ry me home.

Melody lines

Mango walk

My bro- ther did- a tell me that you go man- go walk, you go man- go walk, you go man- go walk, my

bro- ther did- a tell me that you go man- go walk and steal all the num - ber 'lev - en.

Sarasponda

Sa - ra - spon- da, sa - ra- spon- da, sa - ra - spon- da, ret, set, set. Sa - ra- spon- da, sa - ra- spon- da, sa - ra-

spon- da, ret, set, set. A - do - ray - oh!: A - do - ray boom- day - oh! A -

do - ray boom- day ret, set, set. A - say pas - say oh!

What shall we play?

What shall we play in our mu - sic les - son? What shall we play in our mu - sic les - son?

What shall we play in our mu - sic les - son? Glock - en - spiels and chime bars.

Drums, tam - bou - rines and wood blocks, Drums, tam - bou - rines and wood blocks,

Drums, tam - bou - rines and wood blocks, Glock - en - spiels and chime bars.

Melody lines

John Brown's brother

John Brown's bro-ther ran from here to Tim-buk - tu, John Brown's bro-ther ran from here to Tim- buk - tu.

John Brown's bro-ther ran from here to Tim-buk - tu, He's the fast-est man a - live!

Run - ning round the Earth's e - qua - tor, Rang_ to say he'd be home la - ter,

What_ a spee-dy o - per - a - tor, He's the fast-est man a - live!

My bonnie

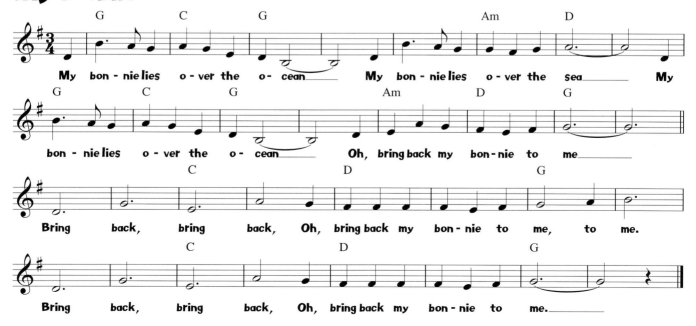

My bon - nie lies o - ver the o - cean_ My bon - nie lies o - ver the sea_____ My

bon - nie lies o - ver the o - cean_ Oh, bring back my bon - nie to me_____

Bring back, bring back, Oh, bring back my bon - nie to me, to me.

Bring back, bring back, Oh, bring back my bon - nie to me._____

Melody lines

Simple gifts

Daisy bell

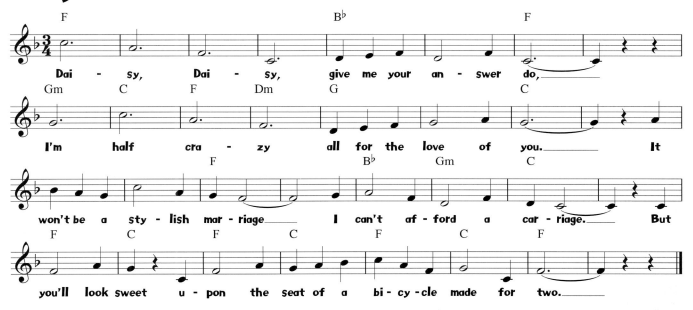

Pokarekare ana

Melody lines

E hi-ne e ho-ki mai ra. Ka ma-te a -hau I te a-ro-ha e.

Greensleeves

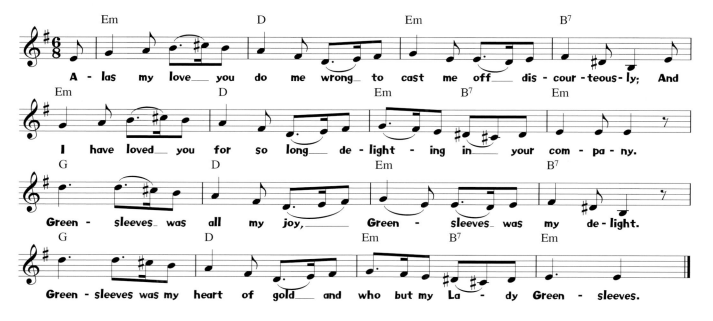

A - las my love you do me wrong to cast me off dis - cour -teous-ly; And

I have loved you for so long de - light - ing in your com - pa - ny.

Green - sleeves was all my joy, Green - sleeves was my de - light.

Green - sleeves was my heart of gold and who but my La - dy Green - sleeves.

Sambalele

Sam - ba - le - le is a mon - key, When he is danc-ing he's fun - ky.

He likes the way he is mo - ving, Friends say there's room for im - pro - ving!

Sam - ba, sam - ba, sam - bó lê - lê, Sam - ba, sam - ba, sam - bó - lâ - lâ,

Sam - ba, sam - ba, sam - bó - lê - lê, Na bar - ra da saia ó lâ - lâ!

Melody lines

Suo-gân

Su - o - gân do not weep, Su - o - gan go to sleep.

When the saints

Oh when the saints go march - ing in, Oh when the saints go march - ing in,

I want to be in that num -ber_____ When the saints go march - ing in.

Land of the silver birch

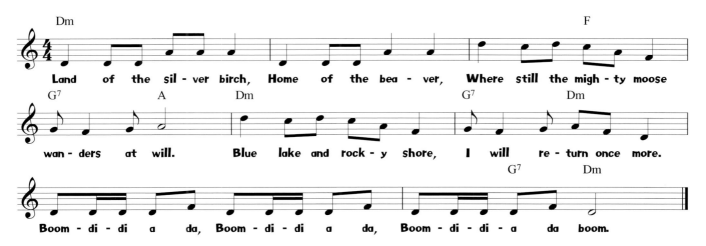

Land of the sil - ver birch, Home of the bea - ver, Where still the migh - ty moose

wan - ders at will. Blue lake and rock - y shore, I will re - turn once more.

Boom - di - di a da, Boom - di - di a da, Boom - di - di - a da boom.

Melody lines

All the pretty horses

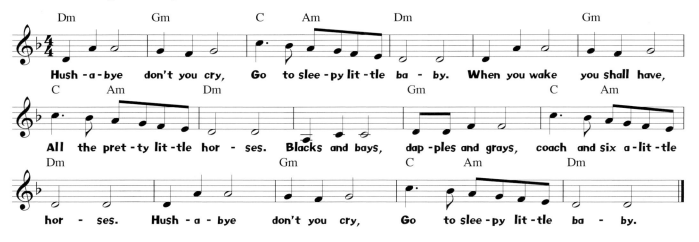

Hush -a -bye don't you cry, Go to slee -py lit -tle ba - by. When you wake you shall have,

All the pret -ty lit -tle hor - ses. Blacks and bays, dap -ples and grays, coach and six a -lit -tle

hor - ses. Hush -a - bye don't you cry, Go to slee -py lit -tle ba - by.

Migldi, magldi

What a fun -ny sight to see, ___ Mi - gl - di ma -gl - di hey, now, now!

A wide o - pen door for me, ___ Mi - gl - di ma - gl - di hey, now, now!

There's the black -smith wor - king hard, __ Mi - gl - di ma - gl - di hey, now, now, __

And his dog is stand -ing guard, __ Mi - gl - di ma - gl - di hey, now, now!

Glossary

Accompaniment
Music which supports the main instrumental or vocal line, eg, the piano music or percussion part which is played while someone sings a song.

Chord
A group of two or more notes played together.

Duration
Long and short sounds, pulse, beat and rhythm.

Dynamics
Loud and quiet sounds, and silence.

Flat
A musical sign ♭ which lowers the note it refers to by a *semitone* (see definition below). When flattened E is lowered to E flat E♭

Interval
The distance in sound between two notes.

Major and minor
Both describe types of intervals, scales and chords. Two notes a 'major 3rd' apart are four semitones (see definition below) apart; two notes a 'minor 3rd' apart are three semitones apart. A major scale contains a major 3rd between its 1st and 3rd notes, whereas a minor scale contains a minor 3rd between its 1st and 3rd notes. A major chord consists of the 1st, 3rd and 5th notes of a major scale, whereas a minor chord consists of the 1st, 3rd and 5th notes of a minor scale.

Pitch
High and low sounds, and in between.

Rest
A silence, or moment during which a performer does not perform. It can be of specific duration.

Rhythm
The grouping of short and long sounds, and silences.

Rondo
A musical structure. The first section (A) is repeated after contrasting sections (B,C,D and so on) making an A B A C A D A structure.

Scale
A succession of rising or falling notes by step.

Semitone
The smallest interval in Western music; it is the distance between two adjacent notes on a piano keyboard.

Sharp
The musical sign, it raises the note it refers to by a semitone. When sharpened, C is raised to C sharp.

Structure
Sections of music and repetition.

Tempo
The speed of the music - fast and slow, and in between.

Texture
One sound performed on its own, or more than one sound played or sung at the same time.

Timbre
The quality of a sound.

Acknowledgements

The authors and publishers would like to thank the following who assisted in the preparation of this book: MES, Gareth Boldsworth, Ron Knights, Cleveland Watkiss, Kaz Simmons, Jocelyn Lucas and Fiona Grant, Sheena Roberts.

Every effort has been made to trace and acknowledge copyright owners. If any right has been omitted, the publishers offer their apologies and will rectify this in subsequent editions following notification.

First edition 2008

A&C Black publishers Ltd

38 Soho Square, London W1D 3HB

© 2008

ISBN 978-07136-84766

Text © 2008 from Jane Sebba's *Percussion Players* series including *Glock around the clock* and *Ring-a-ding-ding*.
Illustrations © 2008 Alison Dexter from *Percussion Players* series including *Glock around the clock* and *Ring-a-ding-ding*.

Sound recording © A&C Black
Cover design © Jocelyn Lucas

Edited and developed by Laura White and Uchenna Ngwe.
Designed by Fiona Grant
Sound engineering by Ron Knights
CD-ROM post-production and interactive whiteboard activity authoring by The Can Studios.

www.acblack.com